This edition published by Parragon in 2012
Parragon
Queen Street House
4 Queen Street
Bath BA1 1HE, UK
www.parragon.com

ISBN 978-1-4454-6632-3

Printed in China

One Bear Lost

Karen Hayles and Jenny Jones

Parragon

Bath · New York · Singapore · Hong Kong · Cologne · Delhi
Melbourne · Amsterdam · Johannesburg · Auckland · Shenzhen

Ten sleepy bears wake from a winter's night.

One wanders out in the early morning light.

Nine scruffy bears wash in a sparkling stream.

One dries off, his fur all fresh and clean.

Eight hungry bears go on a hunt for food.

One wanders off when she
smells something good!

Seven silent bears pad softly through the trees.

One **sniffs** some honey and goes looking for bees.

Six playful bears have fun in the snow.

One disappears – bottom high, head low.

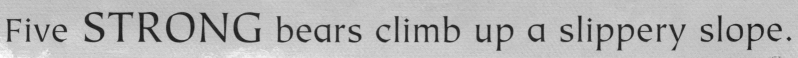
Five STRONG bears climb up a slippery slope.

One slides down. She let go of the rope!

Four weary bears have a rest at the top.

One falls over, *flippety-flop!*

Three lively bears *race* down the icy hill.

One stops to rest, calm and still.

Two brave bears paddle, steady and slow.

One gets stranded. Where should he go?

Nine weary bears have gone back home.
But **look!** One poor bear's left all alone.

One bear lost.

Nine worried bears call out for their friend.

Ten happy bears are back together again.

Ten tired bears are fast asleep in their cosy den.